C000016963

MOTHER WILD

A Book of Mothers' Dreams

ISBN: 978-1-4478-1964-6

Limelight Publishing
Po Box 45, Kallangur
Queensland, Australia, 4503
www.limelightpublishing.com

Lulu Press
PO Box 12018
Durham, NC 27709
United States
www.lulu.com

www.lulu.com
www.limelightpublishing.com
www.motherwild.com

Quantity sales. Special discounts are available on quantity purchases by corporations, associations, and others. For details, contact the publisher at the address above.

Dedicated to the dreams

that keep us wild.

In my dream,
I take a journey within.

I meditate in a forest
and a cheeky monkey swings in.

In my dream,
I sail across the sea.

Destination unknown,
adventure beckons me.

In my dream,
upon a camel I ride.

I explore the desert
with my ancestors by my side.

In my dream, I sip a mysterious brew.
I unwind with my sisters and feel myself renew.

In my dream, I climb high.

I trek through the snow and touch the sky.

In my dream, I surf at night.

I soar on waves under moonlight.

In my dream,
time stands still.
I frolic among the flowers
as my cup begins to fill.

In my dream, I speed through an open space.
I howl as the wind whips my face.

IN MY DREAM, WE SPEED ON VAST OPEN SPACES. WE HOWL AS THE WIND WHIPS OUR FACES. IN MY DREAM, WE SPEED ON VAST OPEN SPACES. WE HOWL AS THE WIND WHIPS OUR FACES. IN MY DREAM, WE SPEED ON VAST OPEN SPACES. WE HOWL AS THE WIND WHIPS OUR FACES.

In my dream,
I paint bold and bright.

Creativity explodes as my
imagination takes flight.

In my dream, relaxation is the goal.
I take time for myself and nourish my soul.

In my dream,
the drums and my body are one.

I dance wildly
under the blazing sun.

In my dream, I stand on stage.
The band lifts me up as I sing out my rage.

In my dream, I go for a deep dive.
The magic of the ocean makes me feel alive.

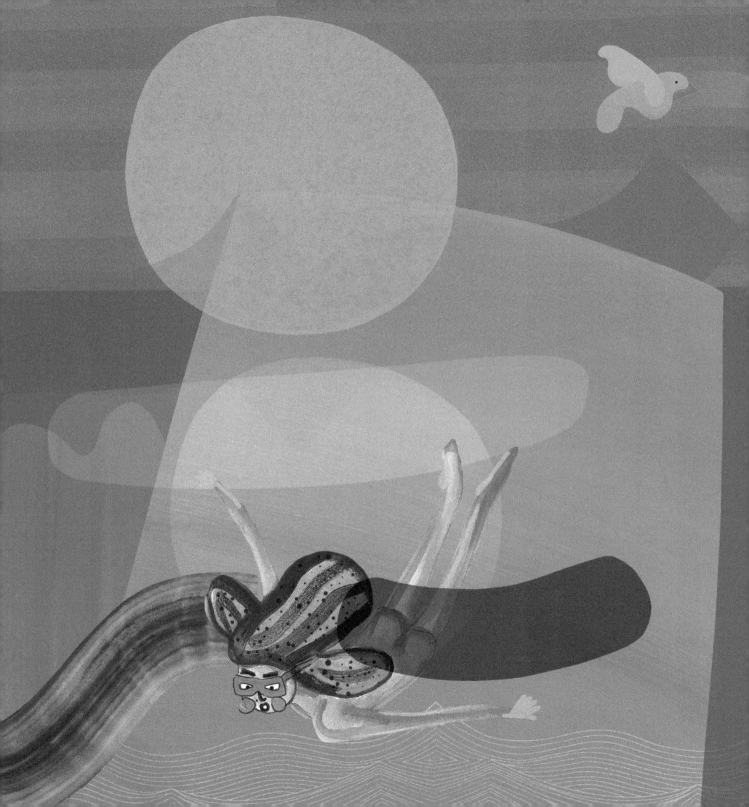

In my dream,
I rest on the moon.

I pause, knowing the sun will return soon.

In my dream,
children run wild and free.

Mothers thrive together in community.

When I dream, I start to awaken.

My wildness stirred by
adventures to be taken.

About the Authors

 Global soul and mama villager Carmela Fleury is French by birth and passport, Spanish by mother tongue, Finnish-Swede by marriage, gastronomically Japanese, and spiritually Balinese.

 Canadian-born Angeli Gunn has wanderlust in her DNA; her Indian grandparents traveled across continents, inspiring her passion for collecting passport stamps with the loves of her life.

 Karin Hesselvik is an Amsterdam-based connector, visual dreamer and big idea generating mama originally hailing from Sweden.

 Anna af Jochnick is a nature loving Swede currently living in London where she gave birth to her third child (and is preparing for the arrival of her fourth) while working on this book.

 New Zealand-born, Japan-based Karryn Miller has spent the last two decades living, working and exploring Vietnam, South Korea, India, the US, and Japan.

 Tasha Miller is most at home amongst tall trees and the open road. You can find her making messes and magic on Whidbey Island in the Pacific Northwest.

About the Illustrators

Beirut-born Niloufar Afnan is an artist and designer based in Montreal.

Deedee Cheriel is an Indian/American artist, filmmaker and musician living in Los Angeles.

Mia Taninaka is an artist and surfer based in Byron Bay.

Argentina-born Guady Pleskacz is a graphic designer and artist residing in Yorba Linda.

Evelien Erichsen is an illustrator, yogi and surfer based in Haarlem.

About the Illustrators

Israel-born, U.S. based Aura Lewis is a feminist author, illustrator and global vagabond.

Nina Egli is an artist and fashion designer based in Zurich.

Lisa Hogg is a South African artist, social impact leader and marketing professional based in Amsterdam.

Lucy Gouldthorpe is a Melbourne-based illustrator and filmmaker.

Mother Wild facilitates retreats, workshops, and a thriving global community designed to support mothers and their dreams. You can learn more at www.motherwild.com